♥ Eva and Baby Mo ♥

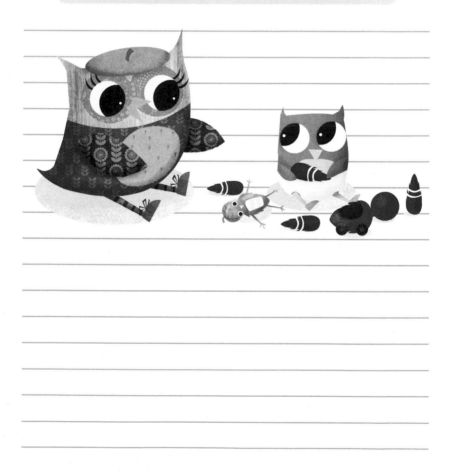

Read more
OWL DIARIES
books!

OWL DIARIES

♡ Eva and Baby Mo ♡

Rebecca
Elliott

BRANCHES

SCHOLASTIC INC.

For all my babies, Clemmie, Toby, and Benjy. xxx—R.E.

Copyright © 2019 by Rebecca Elliott

All rights reserved. Published by Scholastic Inc., *Publishers since 1920.* SCHOLASTIC, BRANCHES, and associated logos are trademarks and/or registered trademarks of Scholastic Inc.

The publisher does not have any control over and does not assume any responsibility for author or third-party websites or their content.

No part of this publication may be reproduced, stored in a retrieval system, or transmitted in any form or by any means, electronic, mechanical, photocopying, recording, or otherwise, without written permission of the publisher. For information regarding permission, write to Scholastic Inc., Attention: Permissions Department, 557 Broadway, New York, NY 10012.

This book is a work of fiction. Names, characters, places, and incidents are either the product of the author's imagination or are used fictitiously, and any resemblance to actual persons, living or dead, business establishments, events, or locales is entirely coincidental.

Library of Congress Cataloging-in-Publication Data

Names: Elliott, Rebecca, author. | Elliott, Rebecca. Owl diaries ; 10. Title: Eva and Baby Mo / by Rebecca Elliott. Description: First edition. | New York, NY : Branches/Scholastic Inc., 2019. | Series: Owl diaries ; 10 | Summary: Eva offers to babysit for little brother Baby Mo so her parents can go to a sky-dancing competition, and she enlists a couple of her friends to help—unfortunately Mo proves to be a handful, eating too much candy, making a big mess, and throwing a tantrum, and she and her friends have to clean up fast before her parents get home. Identifiers: LCCN 2018035372| ISBN 9781338298574 (pbk.) | ISBN 9781338298581 (hardcover) Subjects: LCSH: Owls—Juvenile fiction. | Brothers and sisters—Juvenile fiction. | Babysitting—Juvenile fiction. | Friendship—Juvenile fiction. | Diaries—Juvenile fiction. | CYAC: Owls—Fiction. | Brothers and sisters—Fiction. | Babysitters—Fiction. | Friendship—Fiction. | Diaries—Fiction. Classification: LCC PZ7.E45812 Ek 2019 | DDC [Fic]—dc23 LC record available at https://lccn.loc.gov/2018035372|

10 9 8 7 6 5 4 3 2 1   19 20 21 22 23

Printed in China   38
First edition, March 2019

Edited by Katie Carella
Book design by Maria Mercado

♡ Table of Contents ♡

1	Howdy!	1
2	The Sky-Dancers	12
3	The Mo-Sitting Club	27
4	How Hard Can It Be?	34
5	The Toy Makers	38
6	Babysitting Disaster!	44
7	Trophy Time	60

Woodpine Avenue

1

♡ Howdy! ♡

Sunday

Howdy Diary!
    Yes, it's your favorite owl, Eva Wingdale!

    Let's start off the week with two brand-new lists!

<u>I love:</u>

Fixing things

The word <u>umbrella</u>

Water balloon fights

When Mom cuddles me

Flying loop-the-loops

Singing with
my friends

Winning at
Owl Chess

When Baby Mo
tries to talk

Na ba
na soo ba
woo

I DO NOT love:

Breaking things

The word <u>maggot</u>

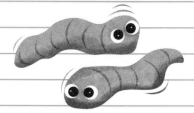

Getting soap in my eyes

When Mom is
mad at me

Flying into trees

Singing badly

Losing at Owl Chess

That Baby Mo can't talk yet

Here's my OWLSOME family!

Me

Mom

Baby
Mo

Dad

Humphrey

On vacation in WINGLAND

And here's my **HOOTIFUL** pet bat, Baxter.

Being an owl is **SWOOPER-DUPER**!

We're awake when the moon is out.

We're asleep when the sun is out.

We can **HOOT** really loudly.

HOOT!

And our wings let us glide through the air!

This is my class at Treetop Owlementary. We all get along well!

Carlos
Jacob
Lucy
Macy
Zac
Lilly
Sue
Hailey
Kiera
George
Zara
Me
Mrs. Featherbottom

Tomorrow is Hobby Night at school. We have to choose ONE hobby to tell everyone about. But I have so many hobbies! How will I choose just one?!

reading
baking
leaf collecting
playing wingball
drawing
crafting

2

♡ The Sky-Dancers ♡

Monday

Hobby Night was super fun! Mrs. Featherbottom shared her hobby first.

My hobby is knitting. I love making big colorful sweaters like these.

We all clapped.

Then it was my turn.
Guess what, Diary!

I chose to talk about you!

This is my lovely diary that I write in every night. Like a best friend, I tell it EVERYTHING! I even tell it when Baby Mo has a really stinky diaper!

Everyone thought my diary – you – were **OWLSOME**!

After talking about our hobbies some more, Mrs. Featherbottom asked us what hobbies our parents or caregivers have.

My stepmom plays the trumpet!

My mom and dad go sailing.

My Dave does pottery!

My mom makes candles.

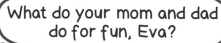

What do your mom and dad do for fun, Eva?

I thought really hard. But I couldn't think of <u>one</u> hobby for my mom or dad.

Um . . . I don't think they have hobbies. But my Granny Owlberta and Grandpa Owlfred play cards with their friends.

I was glad I had thought of something to say. But why <u>don't</u> Mom and Dad have hobbies?

17

I kept thinking about this as I was flying home from school. I was thinking so hard that I didn't see the tree in front of me.

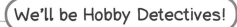

Maybe. Let's make it our mission to find out!

We'll be Hobby Detectives!

We couldn't just ask Mom and Dad why they don't do anything fun. (They might think we're saying they're boring!) So we flew to Granny and Grandpa's tree house to see what they knew.

Granny Owlberta dug out a dusty, old photo album.

You won't think your mom and dad are boring after you've seen what's in here!

Wow!

They look OWLMAZING!

I couldn't believe my eyes. <u>MY</u> mom and dad were sky-dancing champions!

WINGDALES WIN TROPHY

Granny said I could keep one of the photos. I picked my favorite!

Then Granny and Grandpa had to leave for a card game.

Lucy and I flew home.

Your mom and dad look FLAPERRIFIC in that photo!

They really do. But why don't they sky-dance anymore?

Maybe you should ask them?

As a Hobby Detective, it's my duty to ask them!

At bedtime, Mom and Dad kissed me good day.

They smiled as they left, but I couldn't help feeling a bit sad. I'm sure they'd love to go dancing again.

3

♡ The Mo-Sitting Club ♡

Tuesday

Tonight, I showed everyone the photo.

I was wrong about my mom and dad not having a hobby. They used to be champion sky-dancers!

My classmates thought it was super cool. And Mrs. Featherbottom said something really exciting next!

At lunchtime, I could hardly eat. I was thinking about the dance competition. Sue and Lucy were right. <u>Of course</u> Mom and Dad would need a babysitter. But Granny and Grandpa will be busy playing card games. And there isn't anyone else — which is such a shame because I <u>really</u> wanted Mom and Dad to have fun dancing together again.

Then I had an idea!

We just needed to find a way to convince Mom and Dad that we would do a good job.

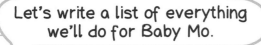

Let's write a list of everything we'll do for Baby Mo.

Yes! We'll show it to your mom and dad after school.

They will love it so much, they'll be begging us to babysit!

Here's our list:

- Make bug candy snacks
- Make toys for Mo to play with
- Plan a puppet show bedtime story
- Practice a song to sing him to sleep

After school, we told Mom and Dad about the sky-dancing competition. They were very excited! But they said they couldn't go because of Baby Mo . . .

Oh, but you can go!

<u>We</u> will babysit Mo!

We love little owlets!

You know I look after Baxter really well! And pets are just like babies.

Mom and Dad didn't look convinced.
So I gave them our list.

Those are all the things we will do
to make sure Baby Mo has fun with us!

Well, this is a
great list.

You three would have to promise to call us if
there's a problem. And Humphrey
would have to be home, too.

Fine. But I'm not coming out of my room.

In that case, yes! You can babysit
just this once. And we get to dance!

Hooray!!

♥ How Hard Can It Be? ♥

At school, Hailey, Lucy, and I told George we'd be babysitting Mo on Friday.

Babies are hard work!

They are?

Yes! I have five little brothers and sisters. And THIS is what happens if I stand too close to them at breakfast.

Oh dear.

34

We flew to Lucy's house after school
to make the puppet show bedtime story.

We saw Mom and Dad sky-dancing outside the window. Dad kept getting his moves wrong. Good thing they're practicing before Friday's competition!

At bedtime, I peeked in on Baby Mo. He was sleeping. He looked so cute! I don't know what George was worrying about. Baby Mo is an angel.

Sweet dreams.

5

♡ The Toy Makers ♡

Thursday

At school tonight, I was telling Mrs. Featherbottom about our babysitting plans when she had a **FLAP-TASTIC** idea!

Tomorrow, I'd like you each to bring in one of your baby photos. I'll mix them up, and we'll guess which photo belongs to which owl!

We all thought this sounded fun.

I know which picture I'm bringing in! It's a funny one.

I wonder if I'll be able to recognize everyone as a baby!?

It'll probably be tricky. I looked really different.

I was super fluffy.

What about you, Sue? Did you look different as a baby?

I've always looked fabulous.

The Mo-Sitting Club met up after school. We collected pinecones, acorns, and twigs. Then we flew to Hailey's house to make toys for Baby Mo.

We had fun testing them out!

Next, Hailey's dad helped us make bug candy. It was yummy!

After that, we practiced singing a lullaby.

Go to sleep, Baby Mo.
Close your eyes and dream.
Dream of sun, dream of snow,
Dream of bugberry ice cream!

Our song will make Baby Mo fall asleep fast!

I flew home.

At bedtime, Dad came to tuck me in.

First, he did some of his dance moves around my bedroom.

I can't wait for tomorrow! I can tell Dad is a bit nervous, but I know he is going to do great at the competition. And babysitting Mo is going to be SO MUCH FUN!

6
♡Babysitting Disaster!♡

Friday

Mrs. Featherbottom collected our baby photos. Can you guess who's who, Diary?

NOBODY could figure out who this baby was! It turns out it's Mrs. Featherbottom!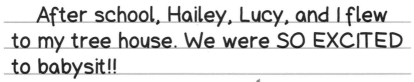

After school, Hailey, Lucy, and I flew to my tree house. We were SO EXCITED to babysit!!

Mom and Dad looked incredible in their dance costumes!

Before they left, they gave us a list.

To-Do:

1. Feed Mo
2. Burp him
3. Change his diaper
4. Snack time!
5. Playtime!
6. Bath time!
7. Read him a bedtime story
8. Get him to sleep $_z z^Z$

But then, Diary, it all went a bit
wrong . . .

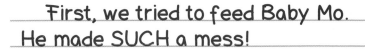
First, we tried to feed Baby Mo.
He made SUCH a mess!

Next, we tried to burp him. But no matter how much we patted his back, he would NOT burp!

Then we tried to change his diaper. But he crawled away!

When we found Baby Mo, he had started snack time without us! He'd eaten almost ALL the bug candies. We took the rest away, which made him HOWL.

WAA WAA!
WAA WAA!

We hoped playtime would cheer him up. And it did. But he started going wild and throwing his toys.

Take cover!

We hoped bath time would calm him down. But he kept splashing. We ended up getting wetter than he did!

We hoped Baby Mo would sit still for our puppet show bedtime story. But he flew off with Baxter.

Finally, we sang him our lullaby. It made Hailey fall asleep, but not Baby Mo.

We asked Humphrey to help, but he wouldn't come out of his room.

So we called George. If anyone knows what to do with little ones, it's him!

George flew over right away.

George shook his head.

And Hailey and Lucy were, too!

I flew around
tidying up.

Mom and Dad came home.

We had a fantastic night, Eva!

Sshhhhhh! MoMo just
fell asleep!

Sorry! You go to bed, darling.
You must be tired.

Mom tucked me in.

Thank you for babysitting.

I'm sorry I wasn't very good at it. MoMo is my brother. I should have been able to look after him better than I did.

The first time I babysat for my little sister, we BOTH ended up crying. You did a better job than me!

Really? Thanks, Mom.

I still feel like our Mo-Sitting Club was a huge fail. But I can't think about that right now. Baby Mo has REALLY tired me out so . . .

7

♡ Trophy Time ♡

Saturday

Hailey, Lucy, and I woke up to the smell of bugberry pancakes.

Thank you both for babysitting. Sorry Baby Mo was sort of a nightmare!

Babysitting was hard work. But it was fun, too!

As we ate pancakes, I told Hailey and Lucy about Mom and Dad making it to the finals.

We tried on sparkly outfits, which <u>did</u> cheer me up.

Then my friends went home, and I went to talk to Baby Mo.

I'm sorry I wasn't a very good babysitter, MoMo.

He threw a pinecone at my head.

The sky-dance competition was SO fun! Mom and Dad looked OWLMAZING on the dance floor. I was super proud of them.

Then the mayor announced the winner. Mom and Dad won!!!

Dad waved the whole family to the front.

The mayor handed Mom and Dad a HUGE trophy. But then – they handed it to me!

We'd like Eva to have our trophy.

It's because of Eva's kindness and hard work that we could dance together again.

Thank you, Eva, for reminding us to have fun.

Eva, would you like to say a few words?

I'd just like to thank my friends Hailey, Lucy, and George. And —

Suddenly, Baby Mo grabbed the microphone and . . .

He burped REALLY loudly!

Seriously?! All that patting on the back and NOTHING. Now this?!

I asked Baby Mo to please give me the microphone. But of course he didn't give it to me. Everyone laughed as my cheeks went red.

Then Baby Mo did something really surprising!

I wuv ooo, Eva.

Oh my goodness! Those are his first words!

I love you, too, MoMo!

The crowd clapped and **HOOTED**.

Let's have a big cheer for my mom and dad!

And for our wonderful owlets!

We flew home and drank Mom's wild-berry lemonade.

I'd be happy to babysit again sometime.

That would be wonderful, Eva. Thank you.

But could you do one thing for me first?

Sure! What's that?

Teach me how to sky-dance!

Dad swirled me around and we danced late into the day!

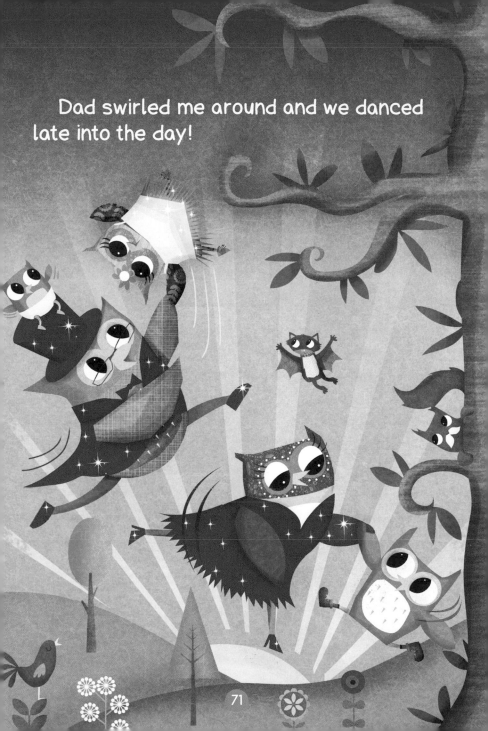

Just when I finally climbed into bed,
Humphrey and Mo burst into my room.

So, Eva, I was talking with Baby Mo and . . .
well, you're not the best babysitter in the world.

Thanks, Humphrey.

But that doesn't mean
you're not the best
sister in the world.
Right, MoMo?

Burp.

I taught him that.

Oh, Diary! What
would I do without
my two lovely — but
weird — brothers?!
See you next time.

Rebecca Elliott was a lot like Eva when she was younger: She loved making things and hanging out with her best friends. Now that Rebecca is older, not much has changed — except that her best friends are her husband, Matthew, and their children. She still loves making things, like stories, cakes, music, and paintings. But as much as she and Eva have in common, Rebecca cannot fly or turn her head all the way around. No matter how hard she tries.

Rebecca is the author of JUST BECAUSE and MR. SUPER POOPY PANTS. OWL DIARIES is her first early chapter book series.

OWL DIARIES

How much do you know about Eva and Baby Mo?

In Chapter 2, Eva and her classmates share their favorite hobbies. What are some of <u>your</u> favorite hobbies?

The Mo-Sitting Club does <u>four</u> things to get ready for Baby Mo. What do they do? Look back on page 31.

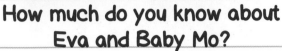

Baby Mo won't go to sleep. Why?

Mo's first words are "I love you, Eva." How do you think this makes Eva feel? How do you feel when a friend or sibling says this to you?

Eva babysits her little brother to help her parents. How do you help out in your family?